India Hamilton
Christmas 2002

CLEO
AND CASPAR

Caroline Mockford

Barefoot Books
better books for children

Cleo wakes,
Cleo winks.

Cleo yawns,
Cleo blinks.

Cleo runs downstairs.

Cleo
hears a
sound.

Someone new
is in the house!

Cleo looks around.

"Cleo, this is Caspar. Come and say hello."

Cleo
sniffs,

Caspar
barks.

Cleo hisses,

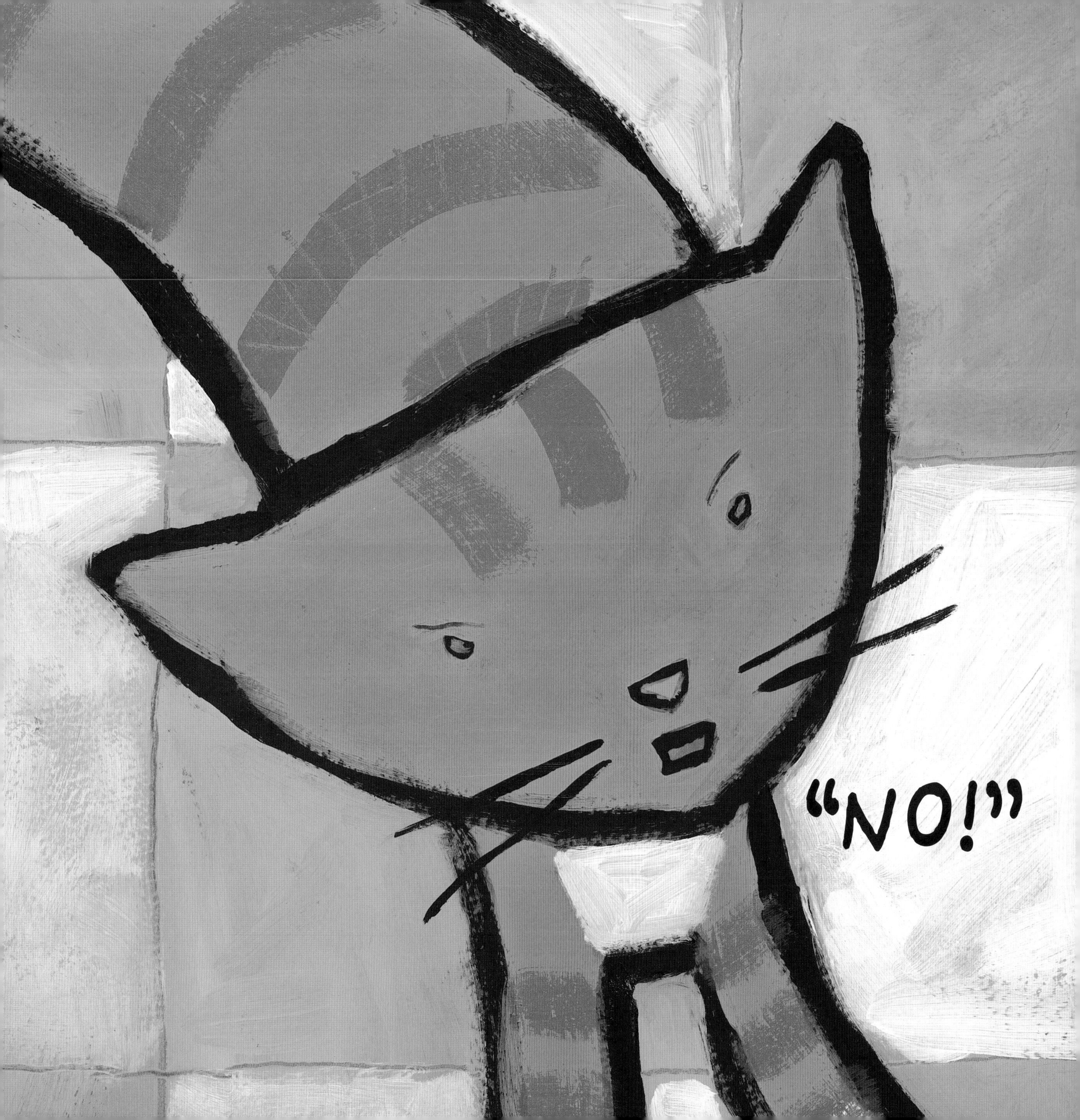
"NO!"

Cleo runs away.

She
hides
high
in a
tree.

"Caspar's sleeping, Cleo!
Come and talk to me."

Cleo comes
inside.
She says,
"Caspar,
you can
stay.

I'll drink
my milk
while
you're
asleep,

Then you and I can play."

For Ellen, Joe and Ruby — C. M.
For my mother, with love — S. B.

Barefoot Books
37 West 17th Street
4th Floor East
New York, New York 10011

This book has been printed on 100% acid-free paper
The illustrations were prepared in acrylics on 140lb watercolor paper
Design by Jennie Hoare, England
Typeset in 44pt Providence Sans Bold
Color separation by Bright Arts, Singapore
Printed and bound in Singapore by Tien Wah Press (Pte.) Ltd

U.S. Cataloging-in-Publication Data:
     (Library of Congress Standards)

Blackstone, Stella.
     Cleo and Caspar / [Stella Blackstone] ; Caroline Mockford.-1st ed.
[24]p. : col. ill. ;   cm.   (Cleo the cat)
Note: The moral right of Stella Blackstone to be identified as the author and Caroline Mockford
to be identified as the illustrator of this work has been asserted. [last page of text]
Summary: Cleo the cat is frightened when the new puppy Caspar moves into the house. But Cleo
soon learns that Caspar is not to be feared, and the two animals become friends.
 ISBN 1-84148-440-7
1. Cats — Fiction. 2. Stories in rhyme. 3. Friendship — Fiction. I. Mockford, Caroline. II. Title. III.
Series.
 [E] 21 2001   AC   CIP

1 3 5 7 9 8 6 4 2

Barefoot Books
better books for children

At Barefoot Books, we celebrate art and story with books that open the hearts and minds of children from all walks of life, inspiring them to read deeper, search further, and explore their own creative gifts. Taking our inspiration from many different cultures, we focus on themes that encourage independence of spirit, enthusiasm for learning, and acceptance of other traditions. Thoughtfully prepared by writers, artists, and storytellers from all over the world, our products combine the best of the present with the best of the past to educate our children as the caretakers of tomorrow.

www.barefootbooks.com